Another Mouse to Feed

by Robert Kraus

pictures by Jose Aruego & Ariane Dewey

A TRUMPET CLUB SPECIAL EDITION

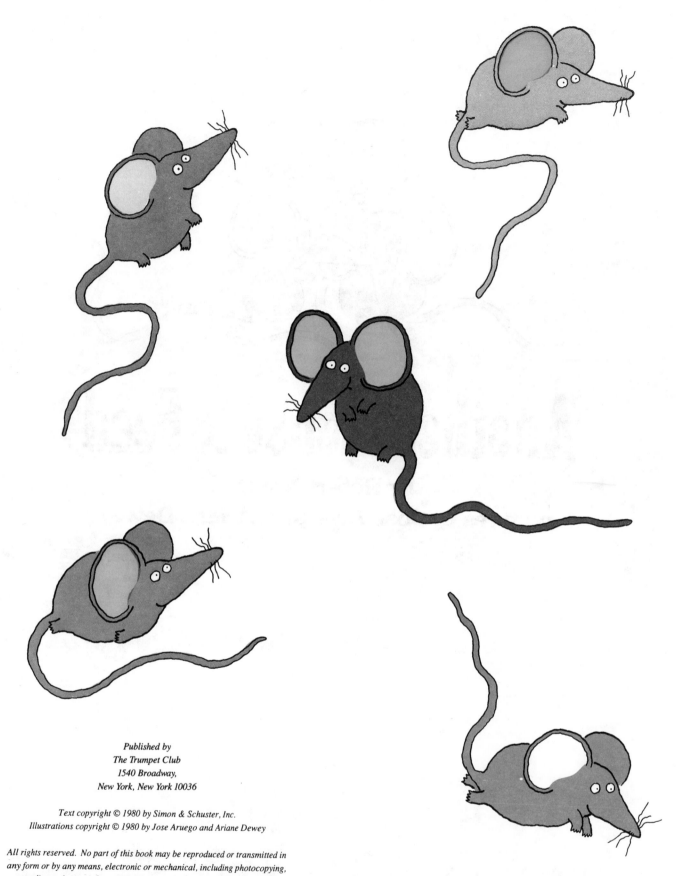

Published by
The Trumpet Club
1540 Broadway,
New York, New York 10036

Text copyright © 1980 by Simon & Schuster, Inc.
Illustrations copyright © 1980 by Jose Aruego and Ariane Dewey

The Trademark Dell® is registered in the U.S. Patent and Trademark Office.
ISBN: 0-440-84548-3

Reprinted by arrangement with Simon & Schuster, Inc.
Printed in the United States of America
January 1989

10 9 8 7 6 5 4 3 2

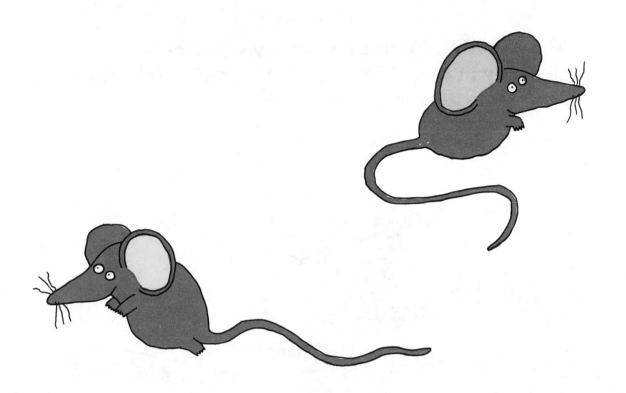
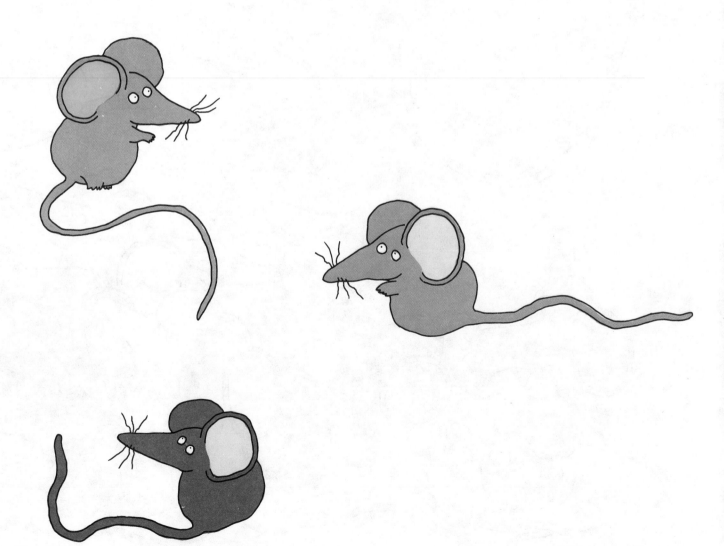

Mr. and Mrs. Mouse had many children,
so many in fact that they often forgot their names,
as well as how many they had.

To help make ends meet, Mrs. Mouse got a job as a roller skating instructor. It was a lot of work, but she never complained because she loved little mice, especially her own.

It was a lot of work for Mr. Mouse too.
In fact, he had to have three jobs to earn enough
money to take care of his family, but he didn't mind,
because he too, loved little mice,
especially his own.

DANGER
MOUSE
WORKING

"I have my hands full with all these mice,"
said Mrs. Mouse.
"I think our family is big enough."

"I don't think I could manage four jobs,"
said Mr. Mouse.
"I think our family is big enough, too."

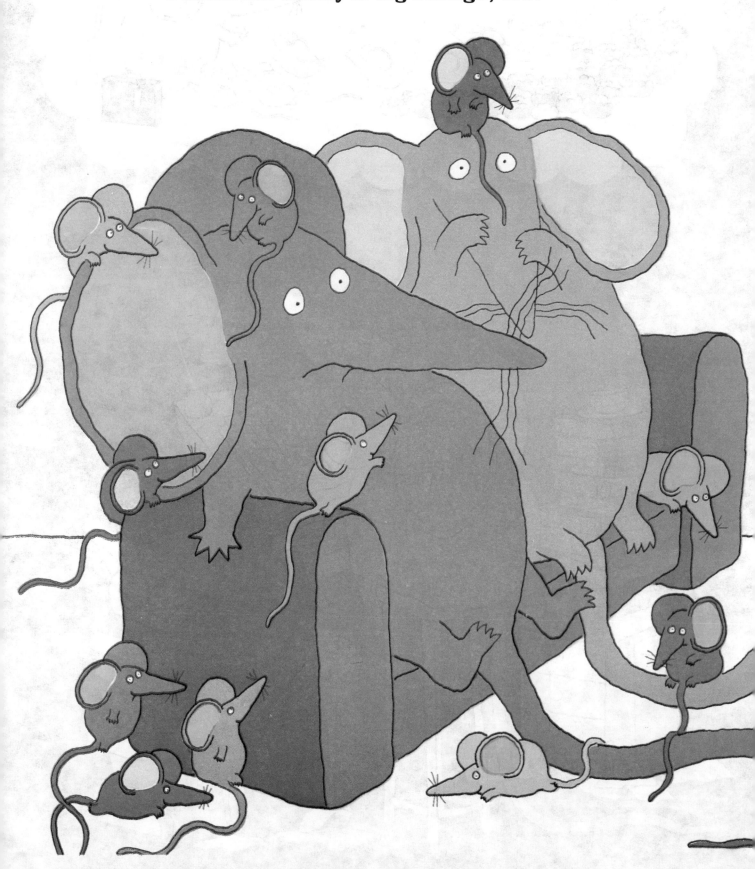

They were just having a cup of tea, when there was a knock on the door.

"Who could it be at this time of night?" asked Mrs. Mouse.

"There's one way to find out," said Mr. Mouse, and he opened the door. And on the doorstep was a wicker basket containing a tiny mouse, wrapped in a blanket. A note was pinned to the blanket, reading: "Take care of my child."

Take care of my child

"A mouse in need..." said Mrs. Mouse,

"...is another mouse to feed," said Mr. Mouse.

All the mouse children were delighted. It was
nice to meet a mouse who wasn't a brother or a sister.

Take care of my child

Mrs. Mouse went to the employment agency to get a second job.

At home, Mr. Mouse started scrubbing clean clothes and stirring empty pots. They were both cracking up.

Edgar, the oldest child, noticed it first,
and he told the others.

"If two parents can support thirty-one children,
then thirty-two children can support two parents,"
Edgar declared. "Dad, you take a much-needed
vacation from your jobs. Mom, you forget
about teaching roller skating for now. Your children
are going to take over."

"But what about your education?" asked Mrs. Mouse.

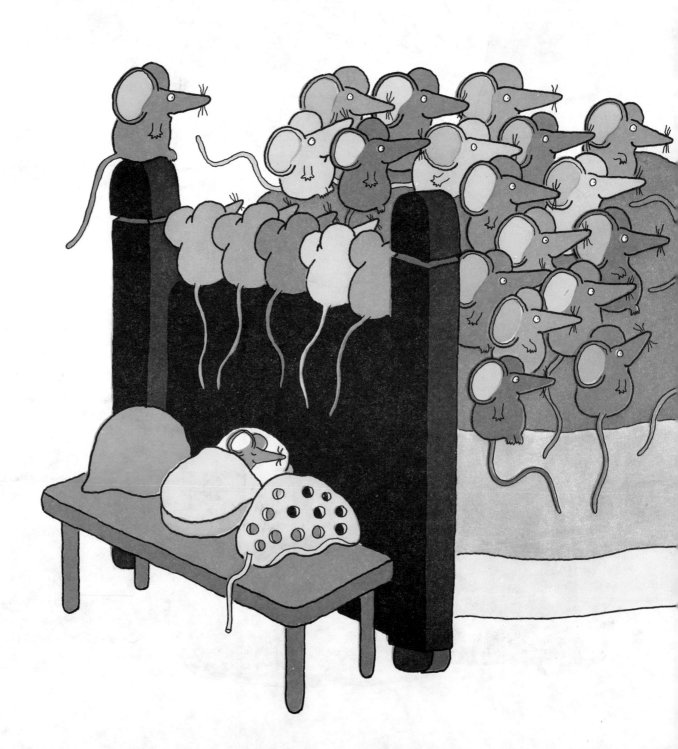

"We'll work after school, weekends and holidays," said Edgar.

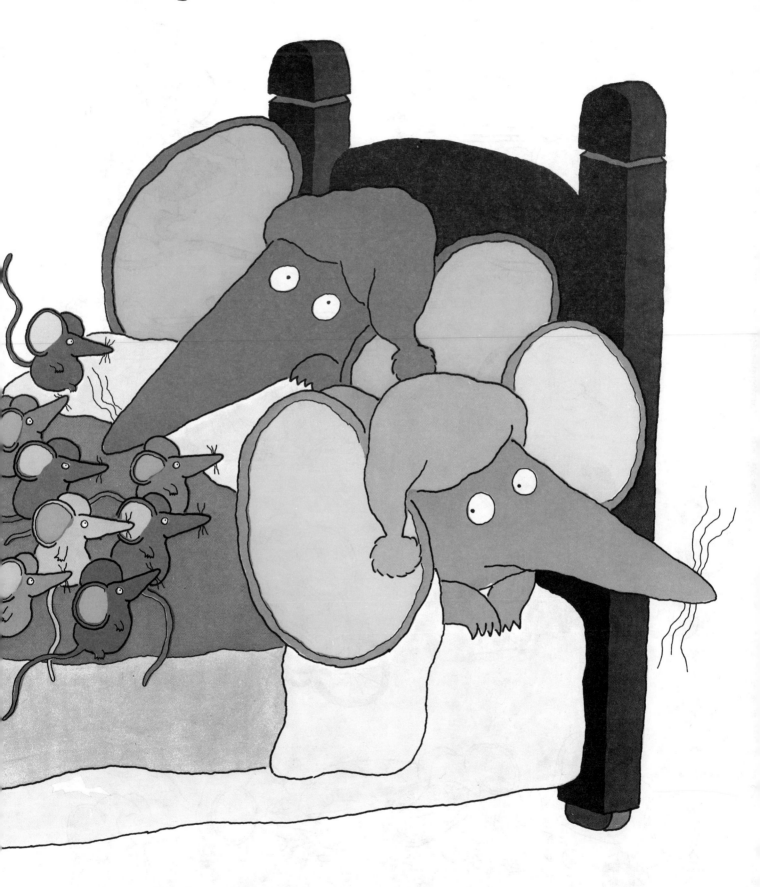

So all the mouse children who were old enough, got after-school jobs,

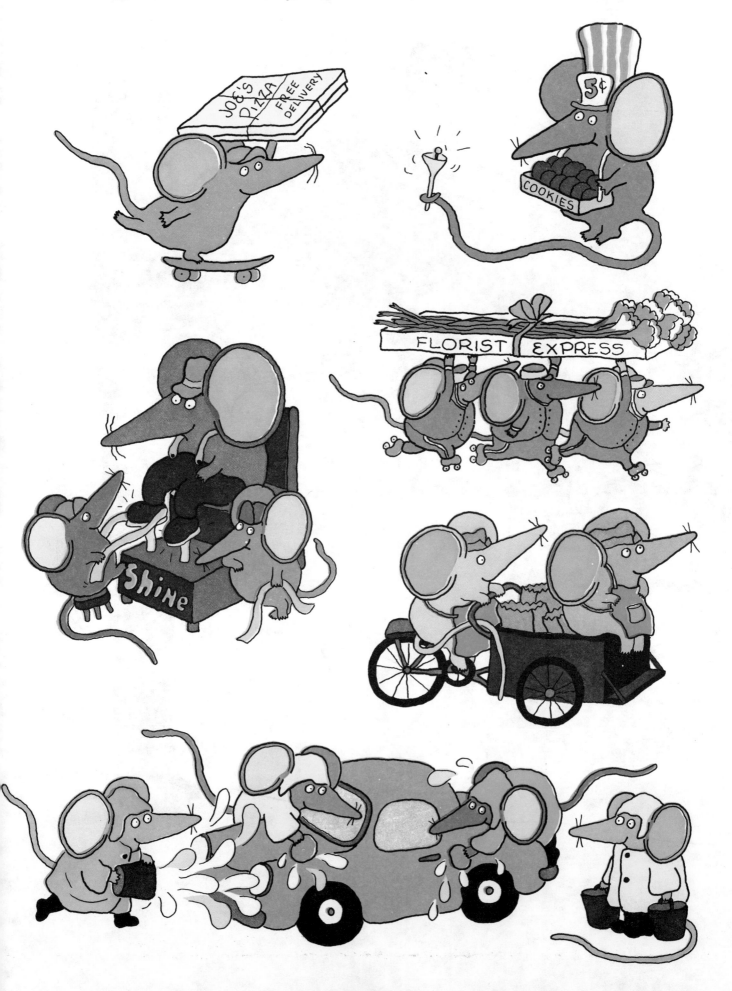

and those who weren't old enough to go to school,
did housework and took care of the new mouse.

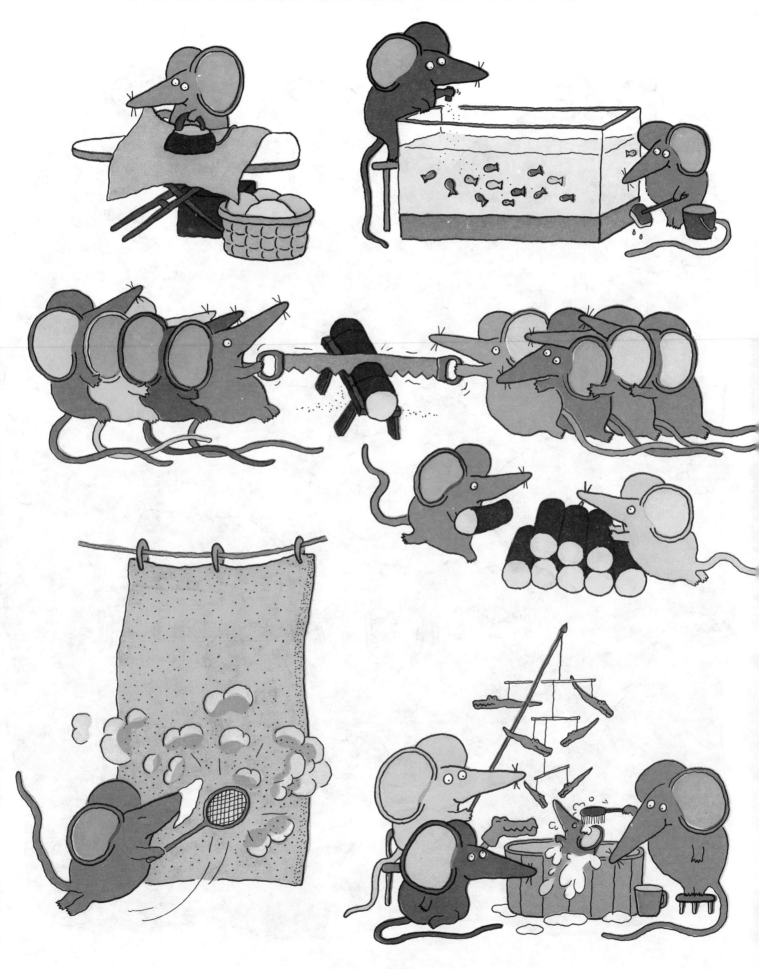

Edgar, modeling himself after his father
got two after-school jobs: delivering newspapers

and sweeping up in a grocery store.

And with seventeen mice cleaning house, it was spotless; with fourteen mice working, the money was soon rolling in.

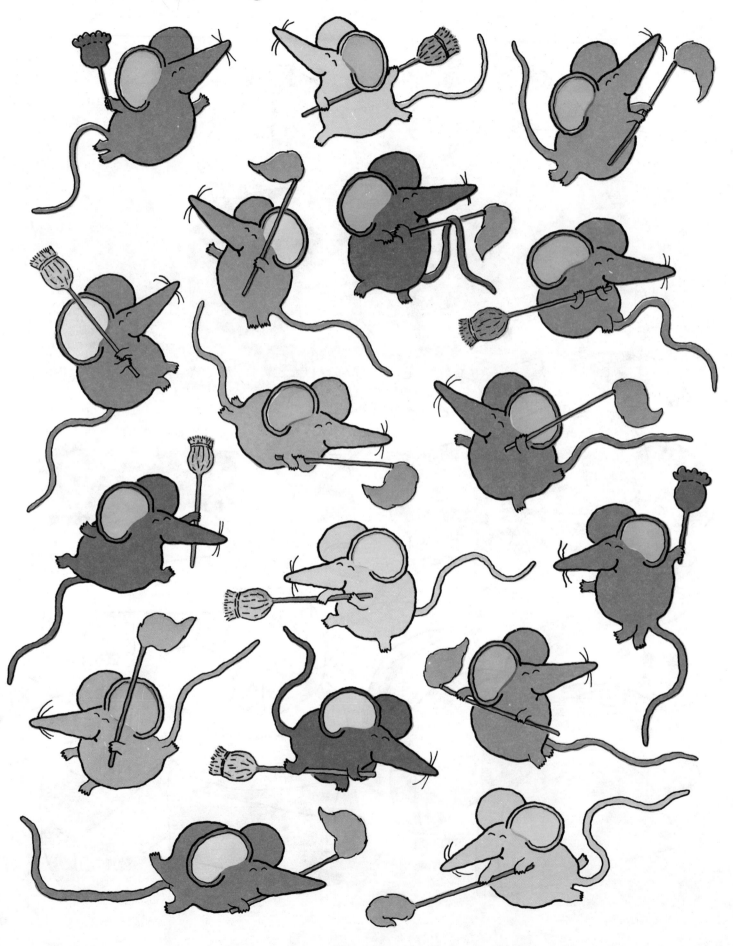

Edgar kept it in cookie jars.
He spent what was needed for necessities and
saved what was left for a rainy day.

Soon, Mr. Mouse and Mrs. Mouse were rested and eager to get back to work. "I'd go nuts just sitting around," said Mr. Mouse.

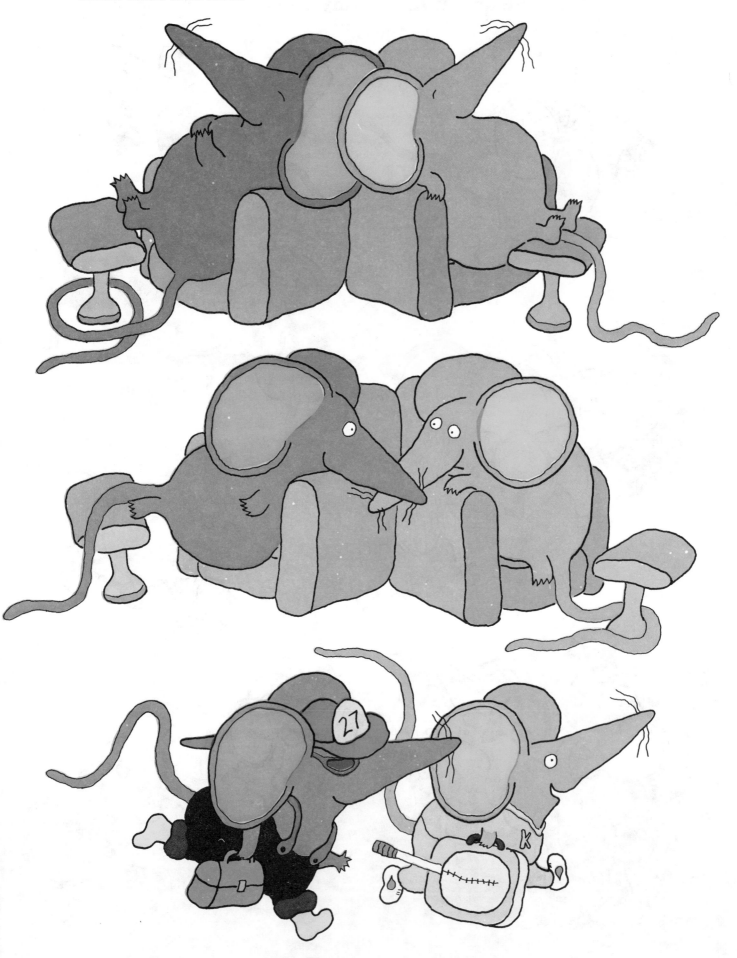

WHEEEEEEEEEE

Mr. Mouse became a Fireman

and Mrs. Mouse became a tennis instructor.

Mr. and Mrs. Mouse also began scrubbing, cleaning and cooking again.

But sometimes they just sat down and enjoyed their children.

All the mouse children continued their after-school
jobs because they enjoyed working, and the
extra money helped.

Before long, Baby Mouse was helping, too.